The Roundabout Bunnies

By Jessica Bentley

This book is dedicated to Mikey and Leo

This book was inspired by Hilsea Roundabout In the city of Portsmouth UK. Growing up in Portsmouth I used to love looking out of the car window while we drove round Hilsea Roundabout and seeing the little Bunnies running around. When I became an adult, I realised that they were no longer there and I wondered why, that gave me the idea to write this story.

In a city called Portsmouth there was a Roundabout called Hilsea Roundabout. It was home to a family of Bunnies; they were the Roundabout Bunnies.

This is Billy Bunny. He is the bravest and wisest of the Roundabout Bunnies.

Billy and his family were very happy living on the roundabout. They could run and play all day and somehow knew to stay off the busy road.

The Bunny family were all very happy.

There were even baby Bunnies on the Roundabout that were very happy too.

But everything changed when the monsters came. They were very tall to the Bunnies and very scary.

The monsters came in a strange metal box that had lots of little doors on it.

They left strange metal cages all over the roundabout.

The Bunnies were afraid and didn't understand what was happening.

Billy Bunny didn't like seeing his family looking afraid. He wasn't going to let the monsters capture his family. He had to come up with a plan.

Bunnies are very good diggers and Billy knew that they could dig a tunnel to get away.

He just had to figure out where they should dig to.

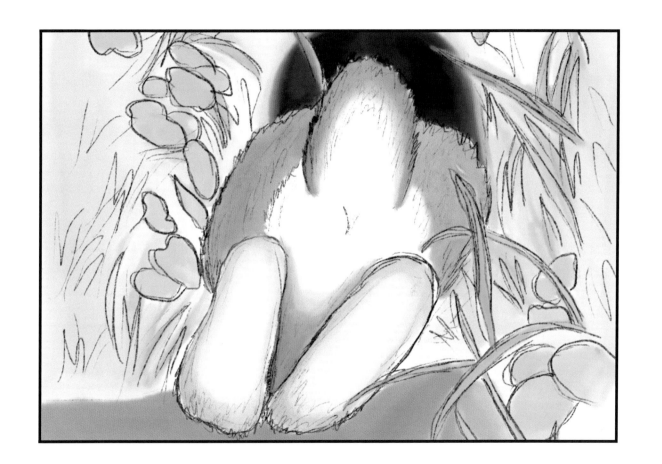

There was a forest across the busy road called Foxes Forest. But the Bunnies didn't really get along with the Foxes.

The Bunnies decided to just dig until they found somewhere safe. It was the only thing they could think of. They didn't want to be captured by the monsters.

They kept digging and digging until they couldn't dig anymore. They decided to have a little peek to see where they had ended up.

To the Bunnies surprise and delight. They had made it to a beautiful meadow with miles of green grass and colorful flowers. There wasn't a busy road in sight.

Billy Bunny was so happy because he knew that they could stay there forever. The Bunnies could run and play all day again and had nothing to be afraid of.

The End.

About the author

I am a writer and illustrator of children's picture books. I have level 3 qualifications in art and design and children's care and development. I was raised in Portsmouth with three sisters by an amazingly strong single mother. I always had a love for art and drawing which was encouraged by my mother and sisters. I take inspiration from my own childhood and from my experiences as a mother to my two children.

Printed in Great Britain
by Amazon